1

Sleeping With the Sun In His Eyes:
A Lost Boy At Home In the World

by Akol Ayii Madut & Bree

Green Panda Press

ACKNOWLEDGMENTS

Special thanks to the many who made this book possible: Matt Jones, Simone Jowell, Thurston Moore, "Whilloughby Jim" Mosher, Ellen Darby, Paulette Washington, Especially Judy, Marilyn Wise, Robert Van Gunten, Erik & Stacy Van Gunten, Al Simmons, Ursula Rossman, Mac's Backs Books on Coventry, Steve and Jane Asdfaervda, Jim and Pamela Shalala, Karen Smith, Sam Salem, Liz Tidwell, Barb Maholkic, Kathy Barile, Andrea Greene, Guy Bauman & Jan Levay, Mom Millie & Kat, Frank and Joan Bauman, Charlotte Mann & Russell Vidrick, and Jim Lang (who wishes to remain anonymous). (Plus whichever h. ache it was had me quit cigarettes so finally during the writing of this).

Green Panda Press

3174 Berkshire Road

Cleveland Hts., OH 44118

Printed in USA in compliance
with the Green Initiative

978-0-9758843-4-8

Memoirish History Sudan Poetry

NonFiction YoungAdult

greenpandapress@gmail.com

Akol wishes to thank Bree, the Lost Boys, his brother (also named Akol Ayii Madut), Catholic Charities, St. Agnes, Father Bob, and Father Mike.

Note: several dialects mean several spellings of the towns and villages of southern Sudan are used in various maps and texts. The authors have chosen the most used, according to their searches.

"All sorrows can be borne if you put them into a story."

-Isak Dinesen, Author of *Out of Africa*

"Never get out of bed before noon"

-Charles Bukowski, Author of *At Terror Street And Agony Way*

Sleeping With the Sun In His Eyes:
A Lost Boy At Home In the World

*

we are all damaged
at birth, bruised
our blood vessels

exhausted, onward we
constantly seek comfort.

that's a poem i started to write before i realized i
was making the prologue to this book. everything's
bordering in on comfort. for the Lost Boys all comfort
was lost with the bombs. their childhoods, smiling with
their families: gone. their books & pencils, beds &
utensils: lost. they were not lost by God but found
comfort painful to remember, painful to forget.
sometimes i think of this when i imagine i am doing
without comfort.

it helps me realize that i almost always *am not*.

in a poem Akol wrote about his tragedy: his wasted homeland and long-gone innocence. in his poem he writes *Everyday I am smiling.* i didn't ask Akol how it is he is smiling each day. maybe because he can. to smile is free. we all are free within our various confinements.

Akol once struck and continues to strike me as an amiable, driven guy. i was and am drawn to his charm and nature. easy-going and passionate at once, he sensibly asks, "Why is it me?"

--Bree   9/9/09

Why is it me? by Akol Ayii Madut

I was born welcome
    to the world
To the womb I was
    Innocent, and welcome

The sun rises—
    all I see is blood
The same blood
    is flowing to the
      ground

Once the villages burned

Nobody is going back now

I look to the sky
    and see black rain
      drops of blood

Why is it me?

I see East Africa—the blood is flowing

I look North and it is the same
   blood flows
as in the
East

No one can speak
to one another

Why me?

I look from the South
and it is the same
   blood as the
East

The West—it is the same

I was born welcome
   to the world

My family was ready to
     bring me to the world

I cried when I carried the gun
I don't have much love
Every day I am smelling blood
What are you going to do?
     Sleep?

I cried out for help
     but I didn't get it

Every day I am smiling
     but it is not enough
for me

*

Sleeping With the Sun In His Eyes:
A Lost Boy At Home in the World

When Akol first arrived in Cleveland, Ohio, and stepped off the plane what he saw was *everywhere wheat flour*. He knew before he came here most American people had plenty to eat. Still he was truly amazed to discover such surplus. Here, he marveled, people left their wheat flour to *just sit in great piles everywhere on the ground.*

Akol wondered if they had run out of the sacks used for holding the flour.

A white woman was nearby working for the airport. He went to her and leant in to conspire in English somewhat wanting:

"I have never seen so much flour. We have people who are starve in my home country. Why don't somebody send some wheat flour back to there?"

"Welcome to America," the woman smiled her brightest at him.

Akol couldn't wait to get outside. Immediately he knelt down to take some of the wheat flour in his hands. The flour was freezing cold! It began to melt away, down through his very grip, making everything wet and cold. His hands, even his knees were wet.

Brrrr! He dropped the melting flour to the ground. This place was unreal. Here in this new city, as it was in a desert mirage, the hulking piles of food disappeared at the touch.

I will be getting used to this and more, he told himself.

He went to join up with his entourage: the local director of Catholic Charities, a case-worker, and a native-speaker—a woman who turned out to be his sister

were among those who escorted the second Sudanese
Lost Boy into cold Cleveland.

999

When Whole Foods opened a store near our
house my husband Brian and I were excited. We love to
cook and are careful about the things we eat and drink.
Call us picky eaters, we prefer fresh, natural ingredients
and avoid junk in our diets. This is partly from working
in fine restaurants like the one we met each other in.
We'd seen Whole Foods stores together on vacations but
never one in our own town.

We were eager as any to see the place. Even so,
we waited a couple days after the Grand Opening to
cruise the aisles with less traffic. In fact, the store still
teemed with wide-eyed tourists. Everyone pushed carts
around entranced, or stoned, by the visual impact of
great, unblemished abundance.

There were grapefruit segments to sample,

shingles of aged Parm to try and goose and ostrich eggs to gawk at. What struck us most about the visit, though, were these very black, mostly tall and skinny African-looking guys who in every direction we looked were sweeping floors, walking around in chef whites or placing fruits in fine rows with the focus of Buddhist monks or model boat-builders.

There was a striking, almost elegance to the men.

Perhaps this is what earnest looks like, I thought to myself as we shopped.

Even as some of them wore the latest Hip-Hop and urban styles, we knew they were not from here, not our city or this country.

In the car Brian and I wondered about the men aloud to each other. And why hadn't we seen any women? We thought maybe the men worked to send money home and would bring the ladies later. Or, perhaps in their culture the woman does not keep a job but tends to the home.

"No, I think the women all work at Stop

'n'Shop," Brian joked. We laughed like children delighted about a thing. We were piqued.

In the next weeks we liked to count how many of them we saw on our trips to the new store. We even made up nicknames for the men: there was the Prince, the Chief, the King, and (this was not mine, but Brian's) Fruit Bat. We were too shy to simply ask what country they were from. We imagined someday, when one spoke to us, maybe asking what kind of bag we liked, we would start, as if it had just occurred to us to ask,

"Say, you have a beautiful accent. Where is it you're from?"

Brian and I knew it was somehow incorrect to make such a fuss about these guys. They made so much of an impression on us we could not help ourselves. The men were striking. Their skin often was like eggplants in color. Their teeth were so white as to give off light, and we noticed, often missing prominently from the bottom row. Some of their whites of the eyes were entirely red. One man we saw had sort of triangular markings, open obtuse angles indelibly drawn on his forehead. Some men towered altogether, above Brian's six-foot frame.

About a year after the Whole Foods opened I turned thirty and as is the fashion found it fitting to make big changes to my life. Among other changes I took a position at the grocery store as a hot bar chef. There, eighteen pans of food were in my man. It was good to be working again with food, something I'd done for many years before taking time to pursue poetry and music while I was employed at both a bookstore and roots bar. Having forged many relationships in those venues, enjoying what felt like a career in passion, I returned the more enriched to my old love: the stove.

I waited until I'd worked several shifts on before I casually, the way out of a night indicated to my supervisor a group of the striking men. Everyone was peeling into the parking lot, and laughing.

"So, who are those guys, anyway?" I asked my supervisor.

We both looked down at our lighters and lighted our cigarettes, fast as fast can while still walking. The cold came in from all sides colliding with, not penetrating the protective heat-layer seven and one half hours inside a hot kitchen builds to frame one's body.

"Those guys? They are the Lost Boys of Sudan," he told me.

"Oh, ok," I said, as if I knew of whom he spoke.

The moment I got home I went to my PC and Googled. Hit after hit brought to light on my screen the same story, of boys orphaned by genocide and other treacheries, walking together with no shoes in the direction they were told, thousands at a time. They traversed deserts, wide gaping rivers, thick jungle and unforgiving bush without food, water, or medicine. They avoided death by lion, tiger, hyena, snake, hippo, croc, bomb, bullet, mine, disease, fatigue and loneliness. They lived at the mercy of a protective rebel army, various outside governments, relief organizations and other authorities, such as their own school teachers, who many times survived with them the systematic destruction of their towns and villages, as they were lucky to be in the middle of class when bombs fell. The boys survived without knowing whether their families

23

did. They kept on, even unsure they'd see their moms or dads ever again. They ranged from five years young to old as nine when they started walking without their sisters. They learned to use guns and to negotiate with them. They outsmarted beasts of burden to win spots at watering holes. They survived by always moving. By the time they could rest for real, they were already men.

999

"You can call us boys," Akol told me, "that is what we are: boys just missing from their parents."

I was headed to the lime-green house on Kerrwood Road in Cleveland Heights, Ohio, shared by several Sudanese Lost Boys. Their place was a mile from mine. It was near enough to St. Ann's Church, is all I knew. Still, it had been too difficult to find on my own. Akol told me the directions over the phone but his accent and "turn left- stop sign -left again- stop sign" directions had me turned around in my head.

Left from where? I wondered. *Which left?*

"You will see a police car, and then you know it is the place, on Kerrwood," he confidently told me.

Police? I thought. *Was this a dream?*

When Akol said "Kerrwood" it sounded to me like "Carroll". This threw me off because we do have a Carroll Road, but it is nowhere near St. Ann's Church.

"Can you spell it for me?" I asked, embarrassed to be lost in my hometown.

"C, no, K," he began, "double R double U-D Road."

Was it a double R or a W? I wondered. Maybe he said double L. It was a mess so I'd had him meet me at the church and walk me.

He arrived in a fishing hat and an explosive purple shirt. The way over he rattled on about nightly pick-up soccer games that took place in the church lot. I could imagine him traversing the blacktop with ease, all limber and long. He told me about a man he'd befriended, a priest at the same church, who was from another African country. It was good, he explained, to speak to someone from his continent. We did not however speak on what we were about to do—mainly because I don't think either of us knew exactly, other than I was to write his story down.

Akol and I had spoken a few times, mainly over cigarettes on breaks from work. I knew from our few meetings that he often traveled to schools and churches to speak about his people, and his life and past. He loved speaking, especially to students. He was a presenter. A writer myself, it occurred to me he should get his story down, have it on the ready to hand out.

One day we were both smoking again. I brought up the book:

"You are already telling your story so often," I justified.

"Why not write it down to give to the students?"

"I have my story in my head, but my English is only so good," Akol explained.

"I could help you with the English," I told him, "plus I am fast, to type."

Akol took a drag and contemplated, his hazel eyes pointing down at the oiled walk.

"Ok, Bree. I will think about it."

And we put our butts out and went back in to work, in our separate departments.

I thought while I buttoned up my chef coat, *this is my chance to write about somebody beside myself*—a rare opportunity for a woman who cut her poetic teeth on confessional poets like Anne Sexton and Sylvia Plath. As a poet my life I had mainly written my perspective, my point of view for the world to see. I was especially eager to climb outside, for a change, as lately frequent bouts of migraines had me wrapped up inside.

I figured I could raise money to print Akol's story. He could tell it and sell it everywhere after; use the money how he liked: to get water in wells back home or furnish his fridge with organic lemonade, whatever.

It was a matter of pre-sales.

What I'd get from it was distraction from my discomfort.

My mind was on the move.

Some weeks later Akol came to me and said:

"Ok, but this will be your book, I want you in it. You will be the writer and I am gonna talk a lot."

"I'm sure you will," I smiled at him.

I'd heard his mouth running before. He wanted *me* in it, and I naturally obliged.

Now I was enjoying our shady stroll beneath oaks and elms on Meadowbrook, winding. The sun was on our backs as we walked, the same as it was on my own as I'd peddle fast on my bike, zooming up the street home as a girl. And, in fact, there was a police car, belonging to a neighbor who lived across the street, parked right in front of Akol's house.

Inside Akol managed to breathe his life story, like fine wine from out of a glass, his long legs sticking out from a long couch. On the couch opposite I hunched and scribbled and manned a digital recorder. In a matter of hours Akol had taken me from his birth in a small village to cleaning corridors in a Cleveland hotel.

I had easily one third of a blank book filled in now with a scrawl that I only could hope would be legible later.

Finally I had a use for the many blank books people like to give you as a gift when they know that you're a writer.

I needed no clock to understand it was getting late. We were done working. Some other boys the night had come in and out, their way to school, or jobs. From what I gleaned four or five of them lived there. But I didn't know, and didn't ask, how many or who.

One roommate named Aleu (pronounced Ah-lay-oh) sat down with us on couches that turned in to feature an enormous TV. I recognized him from the produce department. He was not the least shy with me and smiled all over the place. We talked about Michael Jackson, who graced and had graced about every channel just then with his death and final intrigue. I wanted to talk about anything other than the Prince of Pop.

I asked Aleu how old he was.

"I am 30, to see my American papers," Aleu explained.

"Ha! Then I am oldest in the room." I smiled, since this was an increasingly less-rare occurrence for me. Akol was just 29.

"I am thirty-one," I crowed.

"But I am 35 in my country," Aleu protested, all big eyes and brow.

He was being playful and I decided right away I liked this guy.

"This is America, baby. I am so much older than you," I rubbed it in.

We laughed.

I looked over at Akol, whose smile looked sleepy. I wondered at the horrors he'd revealed to me that night. I knew for one he slept just a couple hours at a time to be woken in the middle of dreams by restlessness, nights.

Like many Lost Boys he would still be suffering memories, missing his family, with war images flickering in his bedroom light. He was too polite to kick me out. I took it for granted that he was now my brother and that we had ignited somehow each other. Content with that kind of security I blew out the light on our evening, and headed home.

999

In Sudan Dinkas don't worry about the day you were born the way we do here. In America we are born on October 29th or November 19th. We are Scorpio or Sagittarius. In Sudan the family of a child born last fall would say he was born 'when Obama won the U.S. presidency', or 'when McCain lost the U.S. election'. Akol Ayii Madut from southern Sudan says his birthday is January 1st. Like most Lost Boys who came to

31

America relief workers assigned him this easiest to remember birthday.

At home *Akol* means 'the sun'. Indeed he was born when the sun began to rise, at about 6 a.m. Arguably, he was born the first strike of the sun, the first day of the first month of the year 1980.

Akol was the only boy with nine sisters; the last of his mother's ten children. His mother *Dock* (the bed of a duck) *Garang* (Eve) *Akol* was seventeenth of twenty wives who lived in close-together homes in the developed town named Kuacjok, of Gogrial West County in the Northern Bahr El Ghazal region of southern Sudan. Eve is also *Aeook*, and refers to women in general. She was named Dock because her father was fishing the morning she was born and *there were many ducks flying that time.*

Half a dozen of Akol's stepmothers came from urban places. They had education and held office jobs before they married Ayii Madut Ayii, a prominent 'politician and lawyer'. (Of course, the Dinka don't have organized government so much as they collectively listen to the words and will of their elders, and chiefs. In southern Sudan, there is not a number to call in an emergency. Here we call 911 or the police. There they *beat the drum* for other tribes to hear, *means bring the spear.*)

To Dinka *Ayii* is steam, or *what comes out when you put a pot of water on the fire. Madut* is something you use to restrain a cow, a beast held in very high esteem by Sudanese. Cows are the highest currency followed by sheep, goats, chickens and crops. There is also a special art in making the horns of the bull grow a certain way, sort of how some Japanese train the branches of *bonsai*.

There is an important rite of initiation in southern Sudan centered about the cow, or more truly, her milk. Annually young adolescents go to pasture for some months beginning in December and drink only milk. It is they and the cattle alone. They do not seek sustenance in anything else for that time.

The rite is really a competition to see which young man can get the most fat from off the milk. Some young men from each family go, and sometimes take with them some sisters. The sisters will not be competing, but they will milk the cows for their brothers and collect the dung. The dung will be used for making fires later in the days. The young men, like royalty, are not to do any work at all, while they are getting fat.

The fattest contestants hold ceremonial sticks and line up to be examined, season's end. Community or chief leaders come out and judge by stomach, biceps, legs, booty and thighs. Everybody not in the winning line-up dances and claps and prays for who the winner will be. The judges are looking for the whole package, including the pride each young man displays. The drum is beat upon. Prizes are bragging rights, or reputation.

Whichever father sacrifices the most of his families' cows for his son to take for those months has the best chance of fattening his offspring.

Of course, it doesn't always end up that way.

All of Akol's older stepbrothers never won the fattening contest. Some young men go with 3 cows, or 2 cows, and they win, but Akol's father would send like 20 cows with his sons.

His father, holding his head, and shaking it complained to his family with his typically serious eyes closed comedic,

"I can't believe it. What don't I have?"

And everybody, Akol, his mothers and his sisters and brothers were laughing out-loud at his dad,

the *not-really sore* loser. Akol is pretty sure even the
lions forgot to be serious that time.

999

Akol was downtown Cleveland walking around.
He had an hour to kill before clocking in at his job in
housekeeping. He saw a youngish girl crying in her
coat. She was alone. Not near a bus stop, or anything,
Akol wondered why the girl was just standing there. He
went to her.

"Do you need anything, girl?"

She didn't answer.

"Can I help?" he attempted again.

She wanted to know if he was from South
Africa.

She wore pink corduroys, white and pink Nikes and a Weird Al Yankovic (a strict vegan) tee shirt under a thickish white corduroy coat. At least half of her hair was in her face and her eyes were black.

He said, "I am from East Africa."

He stuck his hands out to represent the borders of his former land. He made the shape of Africa, tracing it out in the sun. Then he showed her east, pointing to his left, remaining outstretched hand.

He said, "Why are you crying?"

She said, "Some boys called me fat girl."

She pushed some of her hair away from those eyes.

He told her, "In my country if they call you fat girl they are trying you to marry."

"You're gonna smile," he cajoled her.

"You're gonna have admirers."

Both of them tightened their coats—they were,
after all, downtown Cleveland.

In America people strive to be skinniest but the
Dinka of Sudan see fat as strength and prosperity, means
having. A woman here compares herself to the portrait
of the slender super-model.

"In my country," Akol told her, "You are the
lucky one. If a girl is skinny it only means her husband
or father didn't leave too much food for her to eat. It
means he didn't have enough food to begin with."

She smiled. She forgot what she'd been on
about. Akol offered her some money, three dollars.

"Will you take it for a bus? Some food?"

But the girl indicated she was no longer wanting.
She was already moving fluidly on as somewhere a
polka from out of an accordion played.

Kuacjok, now its own diocese, was in the diocese of Wau. This was a major hub of the big Catholic church of southern Sudan. The church attracted many students from all over Sudan to take middle, high school and university level classes.

Akol slept in Dock's house at night, but spent time in each of his step-mother's houses as well, to eat meals or hang out with brothers closest to his age.

Houses were fifteen to thirty minutes' walk apart, or from Cleveland Heights, say, to Cleveland proper. Houses were really huts only sometimes having windows. They were made with earth like adobe brick homes and had thatched roof materials. Mud and sand and branches.

None of the houses in Kuacjok had cable TV. There were not satellites atop them, or foundations below. Neither water nor electricity coursed through or under the walls. There were fireplaces, and spread-out beds and blankets that everybody slept on together. A house was that much a home.

Brothers closest to the same age stuck together because they could relate the best. They woke and ate and schooled about. They played sports and looked after the cows for their mothers and fathers together. They practiced war games, using sticks and spears. They told yo' momma jokes and generally joked around. They naturally got into some scrapes, as well, with each other.

If Akol happened to get into a misunderstanding with one of his brothers, and went home crying about it, his mother would cluck her mouth. She would not let him in.

She'd open the door to her house; leave it open. She'd step back from the doorway, pointing outward with a stern, outstretched arm and say to Akol,

"You go back. Get that boy, work it out."

Akol and the boy would need to be making peace ASAP. They'd come back together holding hands and present themselves to Dock in this way. The boys would close the door when they arrived so his mother knew the fight was over.

Akol had easily more than sixty brothers and sisters but it is impossible to know the number *because all of this time has passed, and the war broke up everyone.*

They all went together to a private Catholic school, by grade. They wore a uniform of white shirts, black shorts, and black shoes. When they made it to high school they would get to wear long black pants in place of the shorts.

Akol's dream was to study to become a medical nurse. He wanted to help people to feel at home as they got better—or didn't. He and his brothers were all taught in the house as well as at school so they learned in both English and Arabic. Akol made it through the fifth grade in English and eighth grade in Arabic before the day his school was bombed from out of nowhere in the middle of class.

That day all the students went running out amid smoking buildings. No place was safe. Everything was streaming wildly. Everywhere was fire and blood. Everybody went reeling, in confusion. Akol was so afraid he climbed into a tree.

Akol and I went to go pick up Aleu from work. We sat in the employee lot when I noticed a guy from the kitchen getting out of his car. I gave a big shout and smile from my window. Rafeek came over to the car.

He laughed, "Akol, why don't you give me some of that weed you're smoking?"

"I am not smoking any weed," Akol said.

"Yeah, right. I know you're smoking the *good stuff*, too, because your eyes are *so red*."

"No way man, I am not smoking any weed," Akol insisted.

"Then why are your eyes *lying*?"

"In my country we are not moving around like you do here."

"Say what, my African brother?" Rafeek asked.

"You are not my brother," said Akol with just a sliver of a glimmer in his eyes.

I stepped in, a sort of translator; "They don't have good circulation in their houses, back home."

Akol nodded, so I went on.

"They have to close everything up in their houses to shut mosquitoes and diseases out. The smoke from cooking has nowhere to go," I explained.

"Oh, is *that* it?" Rafeek grinned.

"The smoke gets in your eyes," Akol unknowingly quoted the old Harbach and Kern song.

"*Marijuana* smoke, that is," said Rafeek.

"The smoke to *cook* is why our eyes, *some* of our eyes," Akol said, making his pretty big for emphasis, "are looking red. So, tell me, why are your eyes looking red, man?" he laughed.

"I'm not a Red man, I'm an African American," quipped Rafeek.

We were all laughing. By the time Aleu squeezed himself into the backseat, and me hardly noticing, Feek and Akol were off bantering in what I took to be a long-going argument.

"You are not African American," Akol said, "you are a Black American. I am African American."

"I am a Black American of African Descent," Feek insisted.

"What is the descent?" Akol jabbed.

The sun was high and pale yellow over the Terminal Tower, visible somehow to the way west of us. Across the street loitered a block of rubble left from the initial razing of a fifty-some years old plaza where I'd bought candy and magazines as a middle-schooler.

Never had I sat in my own neighborhood to be so amused; comfortable in a car-lot with people I hardly knew.

The night was very young and I carried no timepiece. The only thing tethered was the stratus cloud view. Rafeek, though, had to head on in to work. The way in he turned around and shot a warning to the Lost Boys, with a sarcastic stab at my 100 pounds:

"Be careful in that car. Bree could beat you both up proper. I've seen it".

"I wouldn't do that," I said, with a straight face to the boys, "because that could be construed as *racist*".

And we went careening big smiles back to Kerrwood Road.

999

Akol stayed up in the tree for days, unable to

come down at all. Even when smoke no longer advertised the destruction of homes Akol could not come down. Even if he had wanted to, it became night: now tigers and lions began to move about unabashed in the dark. Soon it was day again: the government and Arab helicopters started their circling, overhead like vultures checking for meat (or motion) below.

After four days in the tree Akol heard some crying from out of the bush. It was other boys like him crying.

He also cried. Terrible sounds ripped through the chests and ears of all of those hiding. One boy's crying had become a macabre chorus catapulting.

A teacher Akol knew from school heard the cries and approached the bush. He called to the boys in their various hiding places. He gathered them in, and soberly explained they could not go home.

"Nobody is *home* now," he said.

The teacher urged the boys to trust him, and obey. He said he knew where their mothers and fathers were and that they must travel with him as he says in order to see them; be with their families again.

The teacher Aleu Akol Garang did not know where Akol's or any of the other boys' parents were, but he did know many of them died. He had to trick these boys into thinking otherwise or the boys might die themselves, of grief.

"Your parents are two hours from here," said the teacher Garang. By now other teachers had gathered, conversing and nodding their heads in agreement. Some of the boys went to hold their teachers' hands. They held onto the hands of each other.

"We will take you to see them," the teachers said.

"But you will need to hurry and do as we say."

Garang listened to the radio. He knew in Ethiopia the SPLA was stationed, and was offering protection. The SPLA (Sudanese People's Liberation Army) fought the northern Sudanese government, based in the capital city Khartoum, and gave their lives to the protection of southern Sudanese.

The northern Government had teamed up with

the wealthy, light-skinned Arabs who were after complete dominance of the south. They south weren't buying it.

Ethiopia was a Catholic country, therefore sympathetic to the southern Sudanese and its rebel army. The Islamic government of northern Sudan made a powerful declaration: no non-Muslim would ever again rule the Sudanese.

This was not right! The mainly Catholic southern Sudanese people had welcomed Muslims in. They did not hate, or have an agenda against the Muslims. They accepted as citizens and even married Muslims. They carried on as Christians and wanted peace—their long-time attitude towards anyone outside the tribe:

You do what you want to do, and we are going to stay here, doing what we do.

And yet, the government swiped their homeland from them and held it in their terrible hands, raging, threatening to do just what they wanted with it.

What they wanted was Muslim Law, or *Sha'ria*. The kind where the leg cut off is the leg used to kick and adultery is punishable by death. It is violence hard to fathom, *human abuse*.

Of course, religion was only an excuse, a front. When Dinkas and other southern Sudanese tribes refused to take up Muslim practice or abide by such laws, the government used that excuse to bomb.

There happened to be much untapped oil, and other resources in the region the tribes inhabited. Before such resources could be explored or exploited the government and Arab *Janjaweed* needed to convert (in order to control) the indigenous people.

When it became clear conversion of these proud peoples was out of the question, oil more than anything came to mean murder. It meant a war with no winning side. It was oil and religion, in a coconut shell.

Akol was eight years old, so he spoke for the boys.

"Don't Worry. Let's go—wherever you are taking us," Akol told his teachers.

And they set off together to walk. Not using roads, Garang and other elders led several hundred boys stoic in the direction of Ethiopia.

999

I was coming in the break room to clock in for a morning shift. Four Lost Boys in there stood staring at the TV. They spoke to one another in their own language (known as the Rek of Tonj), shaking heads. A girl from my department, Susy, from the couch asked them what was up.

"There was a big battle in my country, where we lived," one of the *boys*, a utility guy likely to be older than Susy or I was, explained.

"Who won?" Susy asked.

Anthony, who washed dishes for the kitchen, shook his head with an ironic smile:

"Nobody."

"There has to be a winner, in a battle," she insisted.

"No winner, just killing," grinned Anthony, big white choppers in a row.

"Well what side killed more people? Aren't they the winner?"

"It's impossible to say," I said, my back turned as I punched my number in.

"Nobody is winning," I said, turning around with a shrug.

I looked to the Lost Boys for support.

"Nobody is winning," two of the Lost Boys repeated, satisfied and wearing smiles as if there was humor.

Anthony went off on his own, "Death is the winner, this time."

Later I brought a stack of unclean pans back to
Anthony in the dish chamber.

I asked him, *"Who is winning?"*

999

A Poem for Certain Lost Boys by Bree

At home our mothers used to
Grind the food for everybody
To eat

Here we are dishwashers

We grind the food in
Great disposals

*

999

One of the smaller boys sat down. They all wanted to sit down. Around them drew in the hanging foliage of tiredness. Adrenaline of moving focusedly onward came up hard against silencing strains of the same tiredness. The teacher, too, was a mixed bag. For him when the walking stopped, things in the fore drew in while the background all at once dropped a few inches.

"Ok," said Garang, "You can sit, but your parents are just now cooking dinner."

"You must not rest long if you want to eat with them."

Garang scratched his chest and yawned. He eased into a sit against the smooth of a large trunk of tree. Boys piled into the evening shade around him. This is how the clever teacher had to keep tricking boys into surviving. Promises of simple suppers with family to come had prodded the boys. The group traveled on; into scorching heat, hopes of dinner with mom and dad smoldered into memory.

After two months the boys said they didn't want to hear about their mothers and fathers anymore. They were not feeling like keeping their chins up in this way any longer.

"Let's just keep walking," they told the elders.

Akol had fell back to the tail of the group for a change, dawdling on purpose, a crick in the neck he would call a song but wasn't more than some notes that kept sounding in order, like a waltz does keep beating as he walked. Gnats drew constellations about his darkening countenance. He did not wave them off. He kept focused on just sounds. Crickets and cicadas were competing everywhere he couldn't see to be heard, insistent and steady like the roar inside skulls of those who walked long.

Soon his group numbered close to 600 people, as always they came upon still more groups of people when they walked. Littler groups would form, maybe fifteen people at a time, and broke off from his group only to join up again with other groups later. But it was twenty-seven thousand boys walking.

All of them headed the same, for Ethiopia. They left fields where they tended cattle, lying on their backs in the grass, waving a stick at nothing in particular with an otherwise idle wrist, blowing wind from their lips like a hippo exhausts water from his nostrils, periodic, schools where they studied for the future while doodling in a margin, and homes marked by their mothers' cooking where they saw with unblinking eyes their families stripped of pride, burned alive or taken, broken-down and with cuffed wrists to be slaves.

They learned to sleep days and walk through nights, when it was coolest and easiest to move. They walked however they could and slept as they were instructed: holding close together, boy upon boy. A boy could not sleep with his arm *just sticking out*, away from the huddle, or a lion *might come in, take somebody alive*. A hyena might see an opening to come in; swallow some limbs. For almost three months they slept with the sun in their eyes.

Akol was one of the older boys. He urged younger ones to sleep *still*. It was hard enough for him to find rest, even though he was so tired. He understood when they woke in the night to walk again the number would not be the same. *It would be decreased.*

Boys ranged down in age from 9 to 5. It was quite a job to keep walking. Their small feet suspended from heavy legs sang *Workingman's Blues;* once wrinkled only where the toes met to bend, now mangled by thorns and sharp grasses of the bush later to burn in hot desert sands. They forgot altogether the feeling of comfort. The boys wondered if they would become like their feet: *callous.*

When they walked the teachers would point out which leaves would *make your mouth sweat*, and which could be eaten as food *to be strong, keep moving.* They instructed the boys to never urinate on the side of the road. To hold it instead, for somebody else to drink when they needed water, so everyone could just keep moving.

If they had some meat it was with no knife they did the butchering. An animal to eat would get cooked with its hair and skin. The meat would be shared and nobody was getting full. Mainly people subsisted on unripe fruits, water that collected in footprints in the mud, and in other ways hard to believe.

Eventually Akol and his group settled *somewhere, nowhere*, just across the border of Ethiopia. The place was called Etin. There were no houses because nobody lived there. The Ethiopian government had let station nearby the SPLA, who told all of the walkers to just stay put there, wait for help.

The place would be named Pinyudo Camp. For now it was mainly fields. For the boys and teachers having walked 1,000 miles it was finally time to *stop moving*.

999

Akol came out with my husband Brian and I to a Mexican restaurant. All three of us were off the night from jobs in the service industry. Brian had been working as a bartender for some years at a club named Prosperity. Akol and I 'hardly worked' jobs at the grocer. Bob Dylan says *you gotta serve somebody*.

Our gracious server dealt us water and cutlery while we goggled over the menu, written in Spanish. It was vague which of the three of us ordering knew best what to expect, on the platters to come. We ordered too much food, as it turned out, and had a little to drink.

Akol told us Dinkas in Sudan don't drink alcohol until they are much older than the legal age here, like thirty. I asked if he ever saw his mother or father drink some wine or beer. He just looked at me, like he couldn't believe the question.

"Bree what are you talking about?" Akol smiled.

"My parents never drank. No way."

He explained the moral standard was high. People didn't *just drink* with dinner, to relax or feel lighter. Later Akol's roommate, the Lost Boy Aleu would explain it to me this way: in southern Sudan you don't drink alcohol until your first child is married. At the wedding is when a drink becomes a drink.

There are not nightclubs or dance halls where college-aged people go to pick each other up in southern Sudan. If you want to dance, you can pick up a drum. And I gathered there were plenty of occasions for just that.

I wanted to know how Akol spent his free time
with friends and family back home. His first eight years
had been that of any normal boy, and boys I knew here
enjoyed sports, and playing games.

"Did you play sports, like basketball?" I asked
him, eying his super-long full-grown arms, great by now
for throwing.

"I love soccer, running and volleyball," he told
me, "I really love volleyball."

"Is that how you stay so in shape?" Brian joked
with him, making a muscle in his arm.

And thus came a ten-minute comedy in which
the two of them play-debated who was the more skinny.
Brian standing 6 feet even claimed to weigh just 150
pounds. Akol on the other hand was several inches taller
but claimed to weigh much less than that.

"I am like *maybe* 130," Akol stated, feeling

generous.

"You have a scale in your house?" Brian asked with big lips pursed for effect.

"I will bring it down the stairs when we are home. We will see who is skinny," Akol said.

Akol held out his open hand to shake.

"You are on," Brian pointed right in Akol's eyes.

Brian put his own paw out, as if to shake Akol's, then pulled it quickly back.

"*Psyche*," Brian said, with middle-school inflection.

"Big men move slow—just take Shaq."

I was dying. Maybe the expensive lemonade had gone to the men's heads. When we'd paid and left the restaurant, getting them home to the scale became the first matter of business. It was even quiet in the car, with everybody holding on to his bets.

According to the Kerrwood Road scale, Brian, who stepped on first, came to a grand total of 140 pounds. To be sure it was correct I stepped on it next. I knew I was something under 110 pounds.

The scale read 107.

"Ok, Akol," I said, "The scale is working. Now you go."

And he stepped on. And the scale read 140 to the nose. Akol's eyebrows, not being much more than shadow on a chiseled bone were raised.

"I cannot believe," he said.

"What, that you both are so skinny?" I laughed.

999

The UN, with cooperation from the Ethiopian government began periodic delivery of food to the hungry boys and their escorts. Maybe it was popcorn. Then the residents gathered firewood. They came in and sat, each of them close to the fire waiting for kernels of popcorn to pop. Each boy took a turn reaching in for a single kernel.

They went to sleep after, and their stomachs *would come up*. In the morning the number again *would be decreased*.

Nights several thousand boys all lay to sleep, the ground for a pillow. Days, luck went roaring round rampant as comfort: there wasn't much for shelter, just maybe some piece of plastic to make a roof, and have some bit of shade. Everybody's clothes were ruined as they'd made their way to the camp in Etin. There was no medicine, so if a boy fell sick, they would soon bury him.

Everybody kept close to each other but many nonetheless died of loneliness, missing their families and having no hope left at all. Some boys hid out in the forest, wild foliage making the cubicles seem private. Keeping strong with God in the mind helped Akol survive. All of the boys who survived kept strong in the mind, which way they could.

Even though they didn't need to move anymore they needed to keep their thoughts moving, so they would not stop to rest long on their families.

Time went on. Emaciated bodies got used to moving in light. Everybody was thinking things ought to start *happening*. They ought to be resuming life.

Teachers got the mechanism moving. They divided the boys to live in numbered groups with their elders. Akol was put into Group 4, with his teacher Garang. This group forming was just a way to keep track of all the boys. They were let to mingle most of the time. Since Kingdom Come, education had been so important to Dinkas, nothing would stop those gathered now from having school. Teachers had boys from all of the groups use their growing hands to clear the living grass and brush from a big field that was central to the camp.

When nothing grew there any more the same teachers ordered the boys to walk *en masse* to a river about one hour away. At the river, everybody filled what they had—their shirt or shorts or a plastic, with dirt from the bottom of the bank. Then the boys all hustled back to spread it on the field.

The boys could make maybe two trips in a day. They made so many trips until the field was covered neatly with river mud that baked dry in the sun, somewhat evenly.

Then teachers used the dried-mud field as classrooms. They drew into the ground with sticks like it was a blackboard. All the boys gathered thickly in, sitting in rows and columns and climbing into trees to get a good view of the board, like a checker game with plenty of made kings.

They didn't have things to write with, or any paper, but after class they would kneel and use their fingers in the mud-board to practice what they learned. There was plenty to do, now that they were having school days again.

Soon the Red Cross took over, and began delivering food and other rations to the camp. They gave out beef, in a can. Relief workers told the boys to cook the meat but now how they should cook it. It was up to their minds to find how. Mostly, people opened a can and ate the meat with their hands. Plenty more died from this.

Akol, Dominic and I were relaxing on the front porch at Kerrwood. Akol was on a grey-blue couch while Dominic and I opposed each other on black fancy folding chairs. Though there was a roof awning over us the sun got in good. We soaked up as much of the sun as we could, knowing soon enough would be winter. I was peaced out, babe. The only thing I lacked was a frilly sun-hat.

It was slowly becoming the evening before trash pick-up. Neat piles of rubbish already sporadically lined the curb. I noted a bunch of useable stuff, like the large television on somebody's tree lawn.

I said to the boys, "Man you should grab that TV, see if it works."

"I know a guy who could get maybe 20, 30 dollars for the parts," said Dominic.

"Swipe it," I said.

"If it doesn't work your friend can get the cash, at least."

Akol and Dominic just shook their heads.

"What?" I asked them. "Not something a Dinka would do?"

"No." Dominic explained, "In my country we wouldn't do that."

Akol added, "Our neighbors were the news reporters."

I took it in.

I said, "Brian and I go trash-picking. A lot of people do."

And then I wondered to myself whether it was illegal, or shameful to take a TV off a tree lawn, on trash-night.

"What about this?" I asked them.

"Just sitting here with you…in your home. Would you sit on a porch with a married woman drinking 99cent lemonade, back home?"

"No," they said at the same time.

"I mean, what if I wasn't married?" I wondered aloud.

They gave me the run-down, on *girls*. To court a Dinka girl, or woman in Sudan is a long and sensitive process, full of flirting, sweet promises and background-checks.

Maybe you like a girl. Someone in your family way back may have committed a crime. Since Dinkas are the single largest ethnic group in Sudan, and Sudan is the largest country in Africa, that means a lot of people were in your family once.

If, for example, a family feud in your ancestry ended in murder, not terribly uncommon, by the way, as Dinka are fiercely proud as a people, it will be a remembered thing.

A murderer in your lineage does hurt the chances of smooth courtship.

Maybe someone in your family otherwise disgraced themselves somehow. But if you do like a girl, and with a conscience clear, you will go near to her house and call out to her.

You will stand maybe 20 feet away, (or across a Cleveland Heights street). She will come to the door and see, but mainly she sends a younger sibling over to you, to take in what you are on about. You will bend down, and with your brightest charm, tell the child, while winking, 'I am liking your sister, boy'.

The girl is like to be watching through the door at you, hiding her eyes. The child feeling serious in his role will relay the message. He will run not walk back to his sister.

If you are so bold as to go to the door alone you will not face the door, but rather, kind of looking away, you will send complements behind your back to her.

She will not look at you either, at least not in the eye.

She will tell you to come back another day.

A truly eligible bachelorette might "meet" this way for a little while with nine different guys. She would eventually tell her family which suitor she liked best. The family would take her choosing into account, but would meanwhile make it their mission to discover every bit of dirt and glam they could, about each of the nine suitors.

If the boy she liked most checked out, then the two families would sit down and state the conditions of marriage.

The village, or clan, is also asked for input; *it is everybody deciding.* Like American Idol, contestants are let go, by one by one, not without fanfare.

Then there is the dowry to consider: how many cows? Twenty would suffice, in some marriages. In marriages concerning the more prominent set, it would be hundreds.

At a young age the bottom teeth (between the canines) are removed from the mouths of mainly boys. Normally a few kids have their teeth taken out on the same day. An elder removes the teeth by shoving a heated sharp stick through the gums, and under the teeth. The stick acts as a lever bar. It is simple physics to remove these four teeth. It is utter shock and fire to be the one standing still, taking it like a soldier.

Nobody cries because it would be embarrassing, in front of their fathers.

If a father is rich he will have his son's teeth taken out early. He will announce:

"My sons are very brave. This is why they are choosing to have their teeth taken so early."

Sometimes, in the city, say, a child does not have the teeth removed at all, because the families think of it as a tired, old custom. If a guy likes a girl and wants to chase after her, but he still has his teeth, the girl might cluck her mouth.

"How can I be trusting you?" she will ask.

She will put her hand on her hip, defiant.

"You look like you are lying to me, with all those teeth."

Dinka men take their ladies seriously. They will

tell you, no problem, their women are never joking.

Maybe the guy goes to have the teeth removed. He can come back to the girl, but she might say,

"Now get *the mark*."

And he will need to go and have the marking made on his forehead, a sign, a rite, a marking in time distinguishing for all in the clan that he has become a man, finally.

The marking is a geometric scar that spans the brow. Incisions with a knife are made permanent distinguishers. Many Lost Boys were too young to have had the marking made before they fled the bombs. The rite doesn't take place until a young man is in his teens. Still more were raised in areas where markings are the more scarcely made as modernity unroils.

There are other reasons that love and marriage might not go so easily. Maybe a baby is to be born out of wedlock: the expectant father, or baby dad can give currency to the expectant mother's family, to pay for the damage: the broken hymen. Or, the baby momma pays a steep dowry and is married to an older man in the baby dad's family, straight away.

Nobody elopes in southern Sudan. To go without respect of family and friends is like death. Everybody faces up to everything and in plain view.

"I respect you guys," I smiled at Akol and Dominic.

"Even though you are hanging out with a married woman."

"Oh, I didn't know you were *a woman*," lied Akol.

We smiled. It had become dark without us knowing. We forgot to worry that winter came ever so slowly on to Kerrwood.

999

Akol was taken from the refugee camp Pinyudo

to train for six months with the Ethiopian military: how to be a child soldier. They trained him so he could be a good fighter for the SPLA. They taught him how to hold a gun. How to take the gun apart. To fix the gun, and put it back to work. To keep right: on the mark and in the mind. When he finished training they gave him his gun and a uniform and said, "You go".

And into a platoon he went. A platoon had 30 soldiers plus a Sergeant. In a battalion there were 600 soldiers. Akol's platoon was called the Red Army, Battalion 1.

When a town was attacked the grown soldiers went first, to fight. When the battle was heavy the Red Army, full of young excited boys like Akol was called in next. The Red Army knew only shooting. This was the only work they did and they stayed *until the shooting stopped.*

Soon Akol was a Sergeant Major in the SPLA. He was stationed in telecommunications. He knew enough of so many languages: English, Dinka, Arabic, Kiswahili, Nuer, more. People on the outside called Akol in their varied tongues when back-up bullets were needed, or 'extra' soldiers.

Akol would then tell his commander who got the

bullets, or soldiers where they needed to be. He used Morse code, and secret codes and learned fast to detect trickery.

Akol was eleven years old when he took and relayed these messages. Now thirty, he answers a different sort of call from customers, at the grocery store. Sometimes he takes a call, directs it to the kitchen. I maybe pick up the line.

999

Akol wanted to take me out to eat. He made it clear it was his idea, and he would be treating me, making up for some of the migraines I'd been having. I was beginning to regret letting him in on the secret. Since I had told him I also let it out at work, and to anyone in listening distance. He shattered my dam.

I found it intriguing however, when he told me that a hand of Lost Boys in town also suffered from the ailment. I was curious what all they'd done to find relief, if there was any. All Akol gave me to that note was vague answers, much like what the doctors I knew had to offer.

I was all about going out and forgetting the whole thing.

"Where will we go?" I asked him.

Akol replied, "I am taking you where you want to go."

And since I felt like Asian, we had some.

I picked a place I'd been visiting for years. It was such an old familiar, the owner handed me the menu and told me to seat myself.

I entered first, without Akol, as he was parking the car and had insisted I not wait. I picked us out a booth on the far side of the dining room where some late afternoon sun managed to pour in as out of a rushing fount. When Akol was seated finally, having lumbered across the room like a sighting, it was anything I could do to encourage him to give a gander to the menu and pick. He took off his hat. He positioned his phone. He spoke with a roaming eye.

I knew what I was getting, and was hungry like the wolf.

Akol was yimmer yammering—about solidarity and brotherhood. He explained I was his brother. Needlessly, he justified this hadn't to do with my sex, the more fair. He had my back, was his drift. He spoke deep from the heart and meanwhile forgot to focus.

So the server kept coming back to find out we still weren't ready.

The server also gave some weighted looks. He was more put out by our delayed selection than one ought to be, serving at the dead restaurant hour of four p.m. He was lucky, I knew from experience, to have business.

At the end of our meal, when Akol was in the restroom, the server came back to our table with the bill and handed it to me. I thought that a bit unusual as he had always before placed the check smack, in the middle of the table.

I told him, "My friend will be paying."

I put the check in the center of the table.

I didn't want to use the coarser word bathroom.

I kept it at, " but he had to step away quick."

The waiter nodded with pushed in lips. He turned to go but came right back instead.

"Are you sure he'll pay?" he asked me with more inflection than was necessary.

He wore a big brow—as if I'd not paid—or had ever failed to leave a decent tip before! Me being a neurotic, I took it as a personal stab to my character.

"Oh I'm *pretty sure* he will," I smiled forcibly.

On the way out I passed the owner for the first time since I entered. He tripped upon seeing me again! An ocean of slippery laminated foldout menus splashed away from his clasp. They lay prone on tables, chairs and floor o my. On a fallen one, my eye immediately caught the italicized header: *Seafood Treats.*

I half-smiled, thinking how Akol refused to eat

seafood at all. How he and other Dinkas think on our highly priced crabs and lobster as common vermin.

It hit me then that the presence of my lanky black cohort had maybe upset the herd.

"Bree, is your husband well?" the owner asked me artfully recovering the menus.

"Yes, he is good," I managed through wood.

At home I mentioned it to Brian.

"At the Asian spot today, everybody seemed to treat us with suspicion."

"It felt to me like it was on account of Akol's being *other*."

"Of course it was!" said Brian, always the straight seer.

"People look at you two together and think backwards things," he pointed out as if to a child.

A week or so later I phoned in a take-out order from the same Asian joint. After I listed to him my order, *no carrots please* the owner asked if my husband would come to get the food, *as usual*.

999

Because there was no media in southern Sudan people outside of it didn't know very much of what went on within. Elsewhere people didn't know pre-teen boys like Akol were in charge of moving ammo around.

Nobody back at the villages had cable (or sockets) so there were no TVs, and no news anchors. Reporters from other countries learned some things about the children's plight but their stories were lost in a world of stories.

The Sudanese government, not its people, was in contact with the world and they weren't about to tell how they took down towns and villages. Neither did they brag about the families they burned alive, or captured as slaves. They didn't mention how many boys and men died fighting in a rebel army working against their own atrocities, fighting for what they knew was right. But the U.N. came and saw first-hand kids like this, such young soldiers, and knew it was no good. The U.N. called on the international world for support.

Ethiopia had a Communist government. This is why the U.S. didn't immediately help. In 1991, after thirty years of fighting, the small region Eritrea won its independence from Ethiopia. Eritrea became its own nation, defeating the Ethiopian army, and chasing out the former Communist regime. Rebels overthrew President Mengistu Mariam, and also forced the refugees from safety. After four years living in Pinyudo camp at Etin the Lost Boys were told once more, *Get moving.*

Oil again was a major factor of war, as Eritrea won the big seaport Assab in their battle with Ethiopia. Just now, in 2009, the United States is building a mega-base at Dijbouti, a province of Ethiopia that also hosts a major French military base on the Red Sea where much European and American oil imports pass. The U.S. gives billions of dollars in what they call humanitarian aid to Ethiopia's military (the biggest and strongest in all of Africa.) Meanwhile, the Eritrean military is in range of the new mega-base so that if they chose they could likely shut it down with ease, further angering Ethiopian officials. Still, they fear retaliation from the U.S., so for now there is neither war nor peace between the two nations.

Akol had been keeping busy in the military. He learned of what happened between Eritrea and Ethiopia, but the news soon became ancient history. Akol had fish to fry. For seven years Akol kept living as a soldier. It was nine years previous he was displaced. Now important diplomats—strange-sounding white people who rode around in automobiles wanted to know his story, his name. George Bush, Governor of Texas at the time, came to visit some of the boys and boy soldiers in 1997. Akol's troops welcomed them. A lot of people welcomed them. Bush stood talking to the rows and rows of boys, singling some out with questions.

To Akol the governor inquired, "How old are you?"

"I am seventeen," he answered. He puffed out

tall. He knew he was looking *presentable.*

Bush pointed up and down; indicated Akol's uniform get-up.

He asked, "What are you doing with that gun?"

Akol explained, "I am protecting myself."

"I am saving my mother and my father."

Bush looked to another soldier. He pointed at him saying, "How can I help?"

The soldier answered, "If you can bring peace to southern Sudan that would be appreciated."

There was a rumble in the crowd.
This is the only thing every boy wanted.

Akol had never before seen cars like the one the white governor arrived in. He wondered if there were both black and white people in America.
Akol didn't know much about the United States

but he understood it was a *power country; the only single nation the whole world feared.*

At that time military still was heavily recruited for the SPLA. A boy soldier would train for six months and be sent back in to Sudan. Round after round of boys reentered places similar to their own old haunts. There they would either fight or die. Some would make it back to their own villages, to eke out their living family if the commander of the task force permitted. Akol's commander did not allow such frivolity.

999

Eritrea gave the Lost Boys 24 hours to get going. The bullets, however, started flying early. Lost Boys began walking again. Of course while they walked they were bombed by the Sudanese air force overhead. They avoided bullets shot from deep in the bush by hidden shooters. They met people on roads who pretended to be friends before taking their lives.

Many skeletons lined the paths taken out. Any boy who felt like resting moved quickly along instead, when they came upon such evil markers.

Akol's latest command was to escort boys into and through Sudan. They needed to first cross the River Gilo. The river was only as wide as a Cleveland Heights duplex, and yet it teemed with crocodiles, hippopotamus, and big fish that swallow people whole. Plus the current was strong enough that if you stepped into it *you were going to end up Downtown*, meaning dead.

He and other boy soldiers managed to get big ropes across the river. They held the ropes with all of their strength. Boys climbed on the rope and hoisted themselves, one at a time shimmying or slithering across. Some boys' legs were taken off. Something from the water bit the legs off. *This was up to the boys.* Akol and his soldiers held the rope. Numbers were decreased.

Some rogue boys leaving Etin decided to sneak back away from their groups and enter into towns to get food. Dominic was one of these boys that wrapped food and whatever else could be managed, looting it all into plastic bags. They carried the heavy bags, *thirty? I asked, no fifty pounds,* Dominic told me, with Akol nodding his head, each, on their backs. The bags made okay rafts, to get across River Gilo.

Having made it across the river however they had the boys next had to traverse formidable desert again. This time, they were accompanied by tanks the Red Cross supplied, to Pochella, a lightly populated town in Sudan where the SPLA had a makeshift base.

About four thousand refugees had not made it this far. Now 23,000 boys went where they were told. Again on the way they were trying leaves to eat. If the leaves made a bad taste they spit them out. If the leaves tasted alright, they chewed them how long they could, and swallowed them for sustenance's sake.

To Pochella the Red Cross only could afford to send water. No food or medicine was provided the boys. They drank the water. By now the American ABC was broadcasting their story.

Former NBA basketball player Minute Bol of Sudan kept abreast of the plight and sent a load of money through the UN to get food to the refugees. Minute had actually played basketball for some years in Wau, where Akol was born, and he studied English at Case Western Reserve University in Cleveland, Ohio where some Lost Boys would later be taking class.

Minute was often visiting Sudan. He was unable to forget his people. He married in Sudan and was an honored guest there. He contributed something like 3.5 million dollars in total to the refugees there, giving back from what he earned playing hoops, and appearing in ads.

There was no airport, so the food donations had to be dropped down by parachute. The boys then competed with locals to get their hands on the loaded parachutes.

If locals got the parachutes first, they would "sell" the food back to the Lost Boys, who handed over what they had: their clothes or sometimes their wiles.

Meanwhile, the Sudanese government dropped their own parachutes, holding bombs, not food, and this tricked many people into dying again.

Minute spoke to the Red Cross: the boys were not safe in Pochella. He insisted they be moved somewhere else, this time across the desert to the smaller Sudanese town Kapoeta, where water was in ready supply.

The people of Kapoeta lived very spread out. Periodic dams existed where people and their cattle took their water. The SPLA had won control of Kapoeta and was stationed there, so it was believed everybody would be safe. With water and protection in their sights everybody headed there. The government meanwhile meant to take Kapoeta back so daily they were dropping bombs from the sky. Plus locals there were even more eager to get their hands on any food the Lost Boys got.

The locals had both guns and numbers over the boys. The locals often killed boys who attempted to get a drink of water from the dams. Donkeys, cows, camels, horses and other beasts competed for the same water. Nobody was into the idea of sharing. Many boys died fighting to survive.

SPLA quickly decided the boys could not stay. They sent them on to Narus instead: an area close to the border of Kenya that was small enough that the Sudanese government would not be looking for any boys there.

It was practically off the map.

In fact the refugees were able to settle down for three months in relative secrecy before the Khartoum regime took old Kapoeta. The news traveled, and everyone got nervous again. It was only a matter of time, everybody knew in their hearts, before Narus would be taken too.

The boys were told to move again.

To Lokishoka, known among Lost Boys as simply 'Loki': police and soldiers of the Kenyan town witnessed a migration of so many thousand children, skin and bones.

Officials of the town chose an area of Loki where the boys could wait while they finished negotiations with the SPLA. The rebel army explained to the officials that the kids were displaced refugees, just innocents, who came in peace and needed help bad.

The army said they didn't have power to help the boys, so please allow them to stay here maybe three days while everybody figures out where to send them.

Then the SPLA handed the boys over to the Red Cross. The Red Cross did the rest of the talking, directly with Kenya's president, Daniel Morop.

Just like in Kapoeta and Narus, the locals caught wind of the boys being there, and got wild. Again, the people did not like the presence of boys, and did not want to share land or water. In the three days the boys waited together they were already getting into scrapes with the locals.

Them negotiating decided Kenya would provide the boys lasting and guaranteed safety in a big area called Kakuma, but the land would need to be purchased first. The Red Cross raised monies to buy the boys their land.

999

If Christmas came on the boys, or New Years Day did, they might be selling off their rations, in Kakuma.

This way they had a little money to celebrate more properly. They could sell the beans and grain to buy some meat in town. They'd take in a movie—there was a VCR downtown. For five shillings per hour a boy could take a movie in. They also could go and buy candy to take around to the houses, giving a piece to every kid inside, by house by drive, a sort of a reverse-Halloween.

People in town would be going about cheering,

setting off firecrackers.

You don't have firecrackers?

You take the grass in your hand and put it to the fire; *hold it in the air in front of you.*

It was enough to invite some friends to go out and *just be in the glowing moonlight.*

People would be out clapping and praying aloud in celebration of baby Jesus' birthday. The air sang *Happy Holidays.* There was no Santa Claus. Boys'd never heard of such a thing. There was smiles and community.

New Years *everybody on earth* was going to church to sing. Everywhere everyone was *just beating drums.*

Maybe Akol and his brothers pooled together their rations to sell off, make a feast. They could not bake a cake without yeast so they went with their money to buy some. UN had yeast for sale. To make a cake or buy some meat for people you care about was a *holiday situation.*

It was a good break from beans and oil. Meat was better than millet.

Akol and his brothers would take some of the popcorn they grew in the camp and go buy salt, or clothes with it, to treat themselves. In Sudan it is not what we think of: money.

Try beans, try a chicken first. A goat equals medicine. A cow is the last thing you would be selling. It is worth the most. That's *currency.*

The Dinka don't care what other people do with money. To them economics, like politics, is for the busy-minded or no-mind birds. Dinkas grow their food, raise their cows and harvest and swap among the crops. In the cities they are harvesting daughters, to be career women. They are growing sons to send to school, to learn the ways of things.

Akol saw maybe 6 movies in the 9 years he was in Kakuma. He let me know his favorite American movies so far were starring Jackie Chan, Mo'Nique and Cedric the Entertainer.

999

Akol's plane from Africa arrived in New York City, JFK. Five hundred Lost Boys got off the plane. They were all a bit tired and also overexcited.

Where would they be living?

Who would be showing them the ropes?

Of the 500 only Akol was headed to Cleveland. He carried a small plastic thank you bag that held one I-94 Passport, and two changes of clothes.

From the runway he marched conspicuous with the others. They entered the bustling airport getting many looks. Guides led them to a set of tall escalators. The guide nearest to Akol was also at the head of the branch.

He explained, "You're going to step on this and it will take you down."

"The machine does all the work for you," smiled the guide.

Other boys branched down and off in other ways in Akol's peripheral.

Akol finally decided to focus his attention on the guide, who still gestured to the moving staircase, offering *him* the first ride.

Akol had not yet seen *stairs*, so moving ones were quite the sensation. He put one foot on a stair and was sucked all the way down!

He somersaulted.

He slid and slammed against each step, finding no purchase.

He went down crying, and collided with many people along the way.

Everybody was yelling, "Hey, hey!"

He took a lot of people down.

It was quite a scene he made.

At the bottom Akol knelt a while, to catch his breath. While still kneeling, and squeezing his fist to make sure he still clutched his plastic thank you bag, he said to a man in a white security uniform, by way of explanation:

"I put my foot down and something was taking my leg away."

"I try to take my leg back, it cannot come back."

He realized he could stand up if he wanted to, and did.

The people who rode alongside Akol's calamity were all hurt in minor ways. They winced and examined their clothes in a dramatic fashion. One woman took out a hair comb and began brushing in a frenzy. Many others were cut and bruised. There were people who appeared to be upset on the floor.

Akol looked down to see he had great lashes on his arms, which would leave scars to help him remember. He suddenly felt his arms hurting.

Somebody called 911.

A few people went to the hospital.

Akol didn't go. To EMT he refused service. Akol didn't care about the cuts on his arm. Mostly of all, he wanted to find out what his new home would be like.

He wanted to proceed.

He told Security, "I am fine. Just go now, and look after the other people."

Satisfied Akol was not badly hurt, his group kept branching out.

His own new littler branch progressed to the elevators. The same guide explained it was *this way to Cleveland.* He took Akol's elbow with a hand. With another he gestured to doors in the middle of opening, as if to say 'go in'. Of course Akol had never seen an elevator.

He stepped inside one for the first time thinking, *Is this my new apartment, where I will be living?*

To him the apartment seemed small.

But who am I to complain? He justified while his own lip shrugged.

Meanwhile somebody pressed a key, a number lit up white, and pink about the edge. Other people came in to his room, and pressed still more keys!

These people were not looking at anybody in there.

They walked sideward towards the walls when suddenly the floor dropped!

There was a *ding-ding,* then everybody inside the elevator was dropped.

Akol lurched left.

He lurched right, and grabbed onto the shirt of a woman standing next to him.

He and the woman went down.

Some people laughed.

Others cursed.

Akol's plastic bag rolled to the rear of the elevator.

The woman Akol took down got hold of herself first, then assisted Akol to stand.

There was a round of applause.

Akol trembled even though he was sweating profusely.

A man handed Akol his bag.

Akol managed a courteous "thank you," and bowed to a roll of many eyes. Soon enough the apartment stood still and a door was opening again.

There once more was a *ding-ding*.

Akol met Margene from Catholic Charities on a shuttle bus ride. He would get on yet another plane—except an announcement rang:

"The following American Airlines flights are now delayed.."

There would be no flight to Cleveland because of you guessed it, snow.

Eventually the plane took off. When it did, an old pro, Akol held onto his securely fastened belt. On the other side of the flight Theresa, a caseworker, and Ngor, a brother Lost Boy stood holding up a welcoming sign.

On it was printed his name big:

AKOL AYII MADUT WELCOME TO CEVELAND.

The next adventure was a taxi ride. In Sudan you wouldn't be getting in a car. Akol only got in when he saw Ngor do it. Ngor had been the first Lost Boy to arrive in the city. The whole ride in the car from the airport was cold. Akol saw the heat on the window in the form of steam, but he did not feel the heat.

Ngor didn't put on like anything was crazy.

Akol turned his attention to the buildings that flashed by on either side. He wiped at the window to get a clear view. The sky was only white. On the buildings, on trees was everywhere white too.

The car let the boys out at the Church of Our Lady Fatima, on Quimby. Inside the church was a little better. Almost warm. Alongside the church was a row of apartments named after Father Albert, a welfare advocate known as 'the slum priest' because he had set up residencies for the needy. This is where Akol could say was *home* now. Ngor had been living there already for some time in his own apartment.

Akol chose a ground level apartment to live in so he *would not get lost going up stairs*. American people didn't need to climb as they arrived one or two at a time, to show him how to turn lights on and off, and how to use running water. They told him what crackers were, pretzels and chips. Where to plug in a radio.

There'd been boom boxes back at the camp in Kakuma, but this radio had numbers flashing back at Akol the *time*.

Lights and lamps and radios were easy. Water, not so much. There was the hot and the cold. He knew he'd ought to have paid better attention, but to take a shower, Akol already forgot what they said.

He prepared with his towel, and got his soap ready. That much was key. A comb on the sink. He took off his clothes. That was an obvious next step. He opened the curtain, and turned the spigot, and stepped back!

But so far, only a neat rush of water, a thlusshhh neatly hit the floor of the tub.

He did not remember to check the temperature.

He remembered to pull on the device that was the size of an acorn, and round, that sat centrally above the waterspout.

A fine spray came out, in fact, to hit the wall. Akol sensibly turned the showerhead to be evenly over the tub and then he climbed cautiously into the stall.

The coldest water he'd ever felt sprayed his whole prone body!

Akol and *cold* got along like a house fire. He went running out fast as flames spreading into the living room, kicking knees, he left a big mess of water behind, footprints and puddles. He was screaming: *Ahhh! Ahhh!*

He forgot about a towel. It was only Ngor in the other room, a brother.

Ahhhh! Ahhh! A buck-naked Akol managed through teeth chattering, at Ngor.

His eyes would have said it.

Akol took another brave shot at showering, and this time he turned both the blue and red waters on first, slowly, bit by knob, in increments like that, so he could come comfortably clean.

999

When they who survived the journey arrived in

Kakuma with whatever they'd acquired thus far, they saw again a forest with no houses or shelter. The word Kakuma in Kiswahili translates literally to 'nowhere'.

There were Lost Girls, too, numbering somewhere below 1,000 who arrived. Five or six thousand "lost" would end up in other, smaller camps in Uganda and Sudan. Everybody in Kakuma set to work at once, clearing spaces under trees to make small shade for themselves. They waited to be told anything before they could set up something more permanent than shadows, to stay in.

Red Cross again called to the world for support. IRC, LWF, and other orgs under the umbrella of UNHRC (United Nations Human Rights Council) put up the price of the land. They would provide the food rations: basically one cup of oil, one cup of millet or wheat flour, and one cup of either beans or lentils that needed to last each boy fourteen days.

A boy knew if he ate something at twelve noon today he would not eat again until twelve noon tomorrow. It was very hard to wait but the waiting meant each day he could have some small meal to get him by.

Campers received water as well, a staggering

liter a day meant for to hydrate, bathe and cook with.
Boys might combine their rations and eat or bathe
together. They cooked and had a fire and spent the
nights in common. They knew to keep each other well
meant they, themselves, would survive more easily.

Soon displaced peoples from all over Africa
were coming to live in the camp. They came from
Uganda, Rwanda, Ethiopia, Somalia and Eritrea. They
were families and individuals. Everybody was escaping
war and poverty. Today the camp houses some 74,000
displaced people. Its long been designated by the
UNHCR as a danger area. It is fenced with sharp wire
and entirely enclosed by desert, formidable haven.

Akol eventually arrived in Kakuma with many
boys. He wasn't first to arrive because he was busy
escorting. He was just looking forward to resting when
the UN received he and his fellow soldiers by
surrounding them, with guns pointing. They saw Akol
and others wore their own guns, as part of the uniform.

They barked at the boys, "Drop the guns!"

The boys refused.

The UN said, "We will give you two things, then. *Life* and *death*."

Akol saw they were surrounded. Out-numbered, and even relieved, he dropped his gun to the dusty ground.

The uniforms were taken and the boy soldiers were given normal clothes.

Lost Boys made a deal with the locals living in town, that they could take some wood from the forest and use it to build small houses for themselves, just big enough to sleep inside. Akol used some of the skills he'd acquired to sweet-talk his way into some wood. He and Aleu, who would live at Kerrwood Road, joined a gang of twenty or so like-minded people, some women and children among them, and gang-built a home.

When they hadn't wood the boys built with mud and sand. That took forever. Everybody gathered for the roofs leaves of the coconut tree. The houses would have no windows, no *hair conditioner* for when it was hot. Some boys fashioned tents out of cloth from town, or plastic. They'd make tents big enough for several to share. *Home* was what anybody could manage.

To cook anything meant an arduous process of making a fire out of scant dry wood. When it rained it meant nobody cooked. If the sun still wasn't shining tomorrow, it was *wait another day for the wood to dry*.

There was and is a high incidence of rape and other abuse in Kakuma. A girl might go out to get some firewood and end up going to get raped instead, by locals. Even fellow refugees, people who fled war as the Lost Boys did, demonstrated that they knew a thing or two about wreaking havoc.

While Kakuma was protected by UN, and secure when compared with the world outside its fences, it was little more than a pleasant prison. Corrupt security guards leant to this. They were known among the boys as KK—standing for "kikat kidoku," or "pay me something."

Snake and scorpion bites happened lightning fast. Then it was *a long time dying after that*. Dwindling stock at medical dispensaries meant many people died unnecessarily. If a boy was lucky, he was doled a little fish *to eat the wound*, or a capsule.

Eventually the UN appointed community leaders

from each group to speak to the UNHCR: *this is not working*. Little by little the representatives worked for change.

There were about a dozen classes the boys could take. Classes ranged from Kiswahili to Home Economics. It was proper schools, this time, unlike the earthen floor blackboards of Pinyudo.

Akol showed me some of his old report cards from Kakuma. At a glance it seemed plain to me he didn't really try. There were comments on two of the cards indicating as much, from his teachers. But what I gleaned was Akol kept busy in many ways besides.

Some people from Japan came to the camp with books. Akol helped them in the important, if trying task of building a library. Many other people helped. This was work everybody was pretty happy to get used to.

At first he also was employed as a nurse—at a nearby dispensary. He was diligent. Time efficient. He moved with style even as he hurried one by one to the next ailing person. Mostly he was happy to do what he'd always wanted—that is, until people found out how old, or really, how young he was, not even eighteen.

Then he was relegated to acting.

He worked in a traveling puppet show that went about the camp rhyming and dancing out public service messages related to sexual abuse, birth control and STDs, your basic adult public health, with drums and music, costumes and stage. On the stage Akol cultivated a loud voice that really carried. He found out he was a performer. He enjoyed (soaked up) the crowds.

He thought, *I have brothers to look after my safety*. He wanted to help the *girls* to be safe. On the sidelines he was serious, a counselor. He listened to a lot of girls cry.

999

The stove was another Western-World mystery to crack, or turn on with a click. Some literature the refugees read before coming to America listed many hazards of using fire in the house. Every Lost Boy was terrified of starting a house-fire in Cleveland.

To turn on the stove and cook, to turn it off—*nobody wanted to try it*.

Akol and others staying at Father Albert's house were drinking only Pepsi, at first. They didn't want to heat up any tea or coffee, even in the microwave.

A woman named Lynn came and showed them what was what. How to heat things up. If you ought to freeze or just refrigerate something. How to wash the dishes. That the steam elevating out from the dish machine was harmless, natural. Part of the game.

She told them about deodorant, you name. How to be shaving their face. The boys had never seen such razors.

Fr. Mike from Our Lady of Fatima warned them about abusing the heat. He knew they were not used to anything but equatorial climate, and feared they would mistreat the furnace.

"You leave it at 65 degrees all the time," he said.

But they didn't.

They were unsure how, and were reluctant to even try, turning on the heat. Hence their apartments were freezing. They just up and left. They went walking in the cold, their faces pointed downtown. They figured they would find some place that would let them in, some deli or café warm to sit in, to kill time.

Of luck, Fr. Mike saw them walking when they were only a few blocks out from the apartment complex. He turned them back around. He was smiling. He felt badly that the boys hesitated to use the heat. He wondered if had he been too harsh. Theresa, a caseworker, showed up later to demonstrate how to adjust the thermostat.

999

One of the boys picked up the phone. He twisted the cord in one hand; he said "Hello" into the mouth receiver, *"Hello?"* except nobody would answer. All he heard back was a drone—he lifted it towards the other boys, it was kind of like the sound of inside of the airplane.

Now somebody had to come, show these guys how to dial a phone number. And firstly, what is a *dial tone.*

999

American friends took Akol to a drive-through McDonald's restaurant. His friends told him he would like a Big Mess. They told him he would do well to try ordering.

They said, "When you get to the microphone, someone inside will be asking for our order."

"Just poke your head out the window; tell them you would like a 'Big Mess'."

What Akol got handed back at the second window was a paper bag containing a wrapped up hamburger. The hamburger inside was gigantic. It leaked sauce and was covered in cheese and lettuce and some vegetables he didn't know. The bread was soft. *It* at least was covered in something he recognized: *sesame seed*.

He took a tentative bite, halfway for show.

I am thinking I don't like this Big Mess, thought Akol to himself, as he chewed it fast, to get it down.

He wanted to save face, not embarrass anybody. He didn't think the hamburger tasted like any cow. He yearned for the cassava plant, and okra, dried fish and *real* cow meat. Even the rations in Kakuma were better than this.

He went home and found luck seeing Dominic at work in the kitchen. Dominic was good for cooking. There were the old familiar smells, wafting like at home in the Sudan. Even though he'd lost his appetite Akol filled a small plate and took it to the table where his brothers sat.

999

i had no headache
when we took the
Finley Cane trail, love.

was this because of
the yellow mailbox
we saw in town?

*

This was the poem I started writing on a
Tennessee Smoky Mountains vacation with Brian before
I realized I had the title for Akol's book.

I'd had a rotten headache and was feeling the
effects of the Triptan—a medicine made for the sole

purpose of stopping a migraine.

I was feeling *light sensitive.*

I had to move my hand from the paper and peel away the pen because the shadow overtook the written words.

I could not see to write.

The sun was serious. I decided I would be taking it *literarily.*

999

Like Pinyudo camp in Etin, Kakuma was divided into groups. There were fifty-five groups altogether. Sometimes there was fighting amid the groups, but not so much among the Lost Boys. They made up Group One, as they were first to settle. Group One was also known as "the Minors" because of how young the boys were. The Minors were divided into twelve smaller groups. Also like in Pinyudo, Akol was put in Group Four, his lucky number.

Most groups had more than a thousand people.

Group 4 of the Minors was several thousand strong. At the end of the year the elders assembled all boys into straight lines for a head count.

The elders counted the heads, one through twelve. The counting took forever, all day. If a boy was called 1, he went and joined Group 1. If he was called 4, he went in Group 4. Boys were redistributed this way the end of every year. This is the how all of the Lost Boys came to know each other. Grouped together in the camp, nine years, everybody came to know everybody.

If boys were lucky, when they got mixed up again, they might have in their new group some brothers; friends they'd already made. Of course they did not keep strictly to groups as they made their life in the camp.

Akol had not yet arrived in Kakuma the first time the congressmen came. Teachers spent much time preparing the boys to receive the white men from USA. They taught the boys to say in English,

"Welcome, welcome Congressmen!"

Which each of them clearly rang out amplified by special relish. It was the congressmen, after all, who would soon decide which boys came to America, and how many.

Essentially it was a lottery: each boy's picture was in a pot and the Americans dug their hands inside. They pulled out as many pictures as boys their state would be receiving. Ohio would take 37 boys, it had been decided. If your picture was pulled *you would be getting out of this place*, Kakuma.

999

In 2001 Lost Boys of Sudan first began to arrive in America. An estimated upwards of 3,400 Lost Boys were invited to enter the United States with refugee status. They were to become citizens of USA. Of them only 89 were Lost Girls, because the majority of surviving girls had been sold into marriage or slavery, or adopted by families within their tribe.

They came to places like Nashville, TN, Atlanta, GA, Chicago, Il,, Syracuse and Buffalo, NY, Boston,

MA and Centralia, WA. They came to many, maybe even most big American cities, two and five at a time. They came with little English, eager to absorb all.

The drill was each newcomer was put up in an apartment with three months rent taken care of. In those three months they were quickly assimilated; got used to their apartments and learned to move around via public transportation. They collected bus and rapid schedules. They learned to use a dimmer switch, and memorized local laws and government from leaflets, and stapled handbooks.

Caseworkers and people from Catholic Charities took them grocery shopping. They showed them which foods were nutritious, easy to cook, fit the budget. They provided the boys with fitting, donated clothes. This was no small feat since many of them were over average height.

Boys were given this crash-course in American customs and society, and for the final exam were prepped on filling out job applications. They learned: you shower and shave and wear something respectable, to an interview. *You look the one hiring in the eyes and answer straight.*

Once they had their job, the newcomers were on

their own, or at the mercy of a few volunteers.

The few volunteers were not retreating, at least. Individuals Akol and the others were so lucky to know still call, and pop in to say hello in fine ways, even now, eight years into calling Cleveland home.

"Today if you saw a Lost Boy in Chicago, you could tell him, I know Akol Ayii," Akol told me.

"He would know me. You could tell him it is Cleveland Akol, and he would still remember me."

"There are plenty of other Akols, but I am *Cleveland* Akol Ayii," he added.

In Cleveland there is two Akols, and no lack of Peters. One Peter worked in the kitchen with me at Whole Foods. Now he studies to become a pilot. I loved to hear him speak of life before the war in Sudan.

He told me, "If you see the lion you never look her in the eye."

"If the mother has her babies nearby, you can

look at her babies, but never her eyes."

He had a housecat and laughed at her, at how often she gave herself a bath. He said she was the cleanest creature in the world. I asked if he'd had pets at home, in Sudan.

"Did your family have a dog?" I asked.

"A dog in Sudan? He would be eaten by a crocodile!" Peter spelled it out for me.

Peter talked deep too. Things about war and religion, justified murder…what things he said sounded strange, out of place to we native Clevelanders as we grilled chicken or swept up after a rush.

Of the 37 Lost Boys who were picked to come to Cleveland there are 27 remaining in the city. At least five or six of them are named Peter. That means it is roughly 20% Peter, from Sudan.

"Every time somebody says Peter, we need to say, 'Peter who?' And there is a lot of laughing about this." Akol told me.

Dominic nodded and smiled.

I knew just two of the Peters. Every Peter is his own, and has a story.

Even though all of the Lost Boys made the same exodus; lived in camps before going to live anywhere, almost all of them crossing the same River Gilo—they have their own story first. Dominic for one was captured with his family to be made slaves. People with guns came near to the house where he lived and made a ruckus. Everybody in his family quickly hid. His father went under the bed. His sister went running into the bush. In the opposite of silence everyone watched from their own nooks as men with guns surrounded the bed, threatening Dominic's ousted father:

"Come with us, or we promise we will find all of your kids," they growled in Arabic, dragging him out from under, not without blows.

The present family was taken with no fight to a place fenced in and surrounded by armed, angry Arabic *Janjaweed*: the soldiers trained by more powerful people to move the Dinka tribe out of the way. Dominic watched as his shackled and beaten father held out on the captors. The Janjaweed tortured his father, taunting him in front of his mother. Dominic could not stand to witness the abuse any longer because he knew already what would come next.

He escaped alone, through a hole in the thorn-fence.

He didn't look around.

He was only running heartbeat and air. Nothing before had excited his sense of *hearing* so much—suddenly his inner voice was *for crying out loud.*

He'd lose the bullets of his captors somehow, flying off into the dark. He would meet other boys in the bush and pick up with them, totally afraid. He'd have some pretty thrill-ride adventures before making it to Pinyudo, like the leg wound that ended him up in the 'hospital': Dominic was admitted by the SPLA into *a little house with mattresses in a line where everybody's going to die.* Inside a boy could get one pill, and plenty of milk to drink.

It was milk, if you are asking Dominic, that kept him alive.

Lord knows they all had a mess of good luck

118

like that. Some spent years on the other side of it, as medics doling out a pill at a time. Others shot blindly their rifles into a storm cloud of meaningless motion. Ask a Peter, ask any boy, and they will tell you how they survived: by being together.

Here in Cleveland the Lost Boys remain together. Together is how they survive. Even as they have been here for a very long time already—beginning to arrive by one in 2001—they have their problems to face together: finding and keeping a job, negotiating with landlords or the gas company, dealing with racism and intolerance, finding out how to concentrate on school when there's a bootylicious woman in the developing picture. Teaching one another to drive, or where to find cassava in Cleveland keeps a many Lost Boy busy.

999

Aleu and Akol went with me to eat at a Cambodian place nearby my house. Of course, Akol knew some people who were dining there, a couple, the one of which he'd worked with at a girls' school. It was not uncommon to run into his acquaintances on our jaunts about town.

Akol insisted we merge tables with his old friends. He also ensured the server was attentive plying us with drinks—red wine for the table, soda water for myself. I of course, had a headache.

We all got full on spicy dishes over friendly talk. We found things in common and swapped emails. After supper the gang parted. The three of us headed to my place. I just had the key to my back door, and so we crept down the driveway in the dark.

I was a stranger to the drive since I normally entered through the front door. It felt like I was in new terrain. On the further edge of the drive rogue trees crept into my property. They would need to be trimmed back to the line of the hedge eventually, I noted to myself. They practically grew into my house as they arched in canopy.

I led the gang, traversing the soft muck yard next and then climbing up on the deck, which had no railing, and steps only leading down from the far side.

"Be careful stepping, guys," I warned them, over my shoulder.

I felt like I was on my husband's most favorite show *Lost*.

"I don't want you getting hurt back here in the dark."

Aleu said, "Worry about yourself. We are used to walking in the dark."

"Ha!" I laughed.

"I guess you got *that* right," I told him.

Cozy enough inside we sat around my laptop, looking at sites Aleu eked out, few of them with decent maps of southern Sudan. I wanted to see exactly where they'd spent their childhood. I don't know that we found on the map either of the places where the boys had been birthed or raised. When one of the boys sighted a town from their memory they got excited.

"*This* is where I went to school," he would tell me.

"*This* is where my mother lived."

The boys told me over cold beverages later that they wanted to move from Kerrwood. They had a mess of a heating bill at that house because they hadn't understood until too late how to deal with estimated readings on their gas bill. They were overpaying. Over and again. They thought moving was the best way out.

Brian and I knew from experience as renters a decade previous to call the gas company and read the meter to them over the phone; avoid such trumped up bills. Really, the company was supposed to come inside each month to note the actual usage, but rarely did.

The boys' gas bills from warm months like May and June of this year were incomprehensibly as large as ours had been back in February. It brought me back to when I'd faced for the first time landlords, and utility companies. I too had enjoyed a winter of reasonable heating bills only to enter into almost summer and meet an extraordinary debt, racked up by the pleasure of not using gas. The bills—neither Akol's and his brothers'

122

nor mine at the time made sense.

A simple plug-in fan kept the house on Kerrwood cool in the living room, when days were hot. They used gas only when cooking at the stove. Even if they cooked for the Red Army those months, there was no way the bills were justified.

But when they called the gas company, people on the line would say, "I can't understand your accent," and otherwise weasel out of the call.

Brian called the gas company on behalf of the guys in July, asking them to send a detailed printout of each gas bill, the last 12 months.

That never arrived.

Now it was September. The boys had already been looking a good couple weeks now for a new spot. One spot had required a $100 check as 'deposit' to even *see* the place. Another apartment, big enough to hold the three boys moving, Akol, Dominic and Aleu, had been its own *big mess*. In the paper it was advertised at $1000 per month. Dominic called the number. The woman on the other end asked him his whole name. She made him spell it. Then she wanted to know where he was from.

"I am from southern Sudan," Dominic told her.

She told him, "The rent is $1600 a month."

Dominic blanched. "In the paper it says just $1000 per month."

"That's a mistake," the woman insisted.

"My daughter placed the ad—she was mistaken."

I turned the laptop towards me and typed in the address for Craig's List in Cleveland. I searched three and four bedroom apartments and houses for rent on Cleveland's East Side. I took notes of promising locations. I wanted to help them find a fair deal. As dark-skinned men with thickish accents they would encounter trouble I never had.

They needed a *heavy*. I hoped a skinny white broad like me would do the trick.

One house for rent in University Heights, the suburb the boys and I work in, looked promising in specs, but it did not give the street name or address. I emailed an inquiry. Almost instantly I received a message back!

A woman replied that I'd need to pass a credit check first, before she would even tell me the address!

I may as well be new at this, I thought to myself. And I thought it was a buyers' market! Man, had things changed, since my own apartment-hunting days.

I'd learned my lessons. Regardless of my interference the boys would be learning theirs. They found their own new place shortly, and moved in.

999

"We work hard," Akol said. "I don't have my mother. I don't have my father."

"The job - that is my father, that is my mother."

Akol was speaking to the Cleveland Plain Dealer columnist Regina Brett.

He went on, "For years, we never hear a gun. A gun come up again," he said.

"If we come and die here, what are we doing?"

Akol took a leadership role among the boys in Cleveland. Even in Sudan, Ethiopia and Kenya, he often felt the boys somehow looked to him for support. Particularly, this was because he was older. Also there was something unabashed about Akol, and brazen.

Here he was the second to arrive. He had so far managed to always keep a place. He'd learned fast to negotiate within a job and at every job he held for any length, was promoted.

He started out work at a rubber factory plant making 11 dollars an hour. There he accidentally shut off a machine, and got burned by some dripping molten rubber. Catholic Charities people told him the job was not safe.

After that he worked in housekeeping at the Cleveland Clinic's hotel. He was pretty afraid the first time he started the vacuum! He imagined he had broken the machine and went fleeing into the halls desperate for help. But once he understood the ways of the machinery, and worked independently, it was not without pride that he labored, doling out bitty toiletries and making the beds.

Akol loved meeting the customers and often got great handsome tips for his kindness. A friend of his from Sudan worked in a similar hotel. He got a crazy tip from a kind old wrinkled white man known best as Willie Nelson. A judge from American Idol was pretty pleased with Akol's service. The boys liked to compare stories, constantly meeting celebs.

A supervisor of Akol's, Yvette, spoke plainly to him, from the heart, even though she was his manager. Another woman named Lana who worked above him had known some Sudanese, in London. He came to know many helpful people like these in his line, and considered himself lucky.

He reminded himself, as he cleaned the corridors alone, that while at home his mother did all of the scrubbing, here he was the man for the job.

He kept getting promoted.

He kept pleasing customers, which pleased his boss, and made it easy for him to get other Lost Boys hired. So, he was opening doors both literally and figuratively.

Akol's supervisor Yvette eventually left the hotel to work in an all girls' school. She was pleased with her new position. Akol followed her there.

At the school he was in housekeeping, as at the hotel. When he had a moment free he liked to sneak his way into PE classes where he was very good with the girls. In the gym it was everybody smiling. The school ended up giving Akol a side job as a soccer coach. Again he was rewarded handsomely.

Akol used some money he saved from all of these jobs, plus credit, to buy a big car that was very much like a dream. He taught himself to drive in empty parking lots, using Dominic's smaller, and easier to maneuver car. He got his license in no time and was styling. He was moving up and around. When a Lost Boy had a hard time at his job or struggled in some way, he came to Akol. Akol knew what to tell these guys.

Suddenly they faced together probably the hardest thing yet: the death of a brother. Akol for a rare moment had no words. It happened in the winter. Everybody was getting ready for the holidays. They needed to make a cake and prepare to light up the town.

The Lost Boy Majok really wanted a Christmas tree. That is what he explained to Mary Francis the day before he was shot and killed, while standing, waiting for a bus at St. Clair and Addison in Cleveland on December 11, 2006. Majok Thiik Madut was only 26. He left as many brothers as he'd lived years, staggering in Cleveland.

All of the boys were crushed.

Akol was crushed. In shock and in tears they banded together. They wondered out-loud whether it was worth staying, now. They didn't understand why a man could survive everything to fall for no reason. Their jaws got tired from asking why. The shooter was not caught. Were they still looking? There was no suspect or motive or sense to make of the shooting.

Again the world went streaming.

Akol headed down to the Clinic to identify the body. It was grief all over again. On the way to the morgue a car swung into him with violence. The side of his car was bashed in, and meanwhile the other driver fled the scene of the accident.

What next? Akol had to wonder.

He continued down the road to ID his friend. When the story of the murder hit the papers

Brett ran several articles about the Lost Boys in her weekly column.

According to the column Majok still held his bus fare in his rigor mortis fist. Brett spoke to Akol as well as other boys. NPR also interviewed Akol, and aired what grief and hopes he shared with them. What he found himself explaining many times to his interviewers was how much the Lost Boys in America yet struggled.

It felt good to talk about all of the things happening. Speaking out seemed to make the world slow down.

When Majok was gone and buried many new volunteers came forward. People everywhere in the city and outside of it were reading and hearing for the first time who were *the Lost Boys*. They wanted to welcome and make the boys a part of the community at last. For many, this was the first they had heard of the new citizens. For many of the boys, this was the first they'd heard from the community.

People came forward to sponsor or mentor the boys. Some just wanted to donate money. Others gathered up gently used clothing or bought school supplies for the boys. A foundation was set up, using the address of a local high school on the Near West Side to properly collect funds which would get the boys who hadn't it already citizenship, plus enough money to pay for taking the GED exam. In fact there would be funds to supplement college tuition for boys who sought it.

Currently all but one of the boys has got their citizenship. Many are in college even as they hold down a job or two. While at first they sent some of their hard-earned cash back home, they came to realize it was hard enough to eke out their own living here, to survive. They began to save for future. Some would struggle yet even to find a job or stay very long in one position.

Cheri Wiseman, now Cheri Patton through marriage, was paying close attention to the press these boys were getting. She wanted to help. A newcomer to Cleveland herself, Cheri would be in administration for the new Whole Foods Market set to open on the East Side. She saw Tim Evan's number in the paper and called him at the high school to find out what she could do. The teacher told Cheri the best way to help was to give the boys applications for a job.

She said, "The first door I'll open is for the Lost Boys of Sudan."

Cheri had worked with Lost Boys at the Pittsburgh Whole Foods location. She had seen good workers in the boys there. She felt passionate about lending a hand and told Tim to bring them to a job fair event where they could apply.

Fifteen of the boys started their lives back up together anew in various aprons. They would work in produce, customer service, meat, seafood and utility. They would have benefits, and a 401k. There were maybe two Lost Boys to any department. Akol left his job to go with the other boys. He had been working at the girls' school as a custodian and soccer coach. He wanted to stay together, close. Now he was hired in customer service—a position he figured, that would enable him *to meet al lot of people.*

As in every hellish dip life takes there are bright points—a tree was planted in the yard at Our Lady of Fatima Church, where all of the boys first worshipped in Cleveland. Everybody gathered to decorate the tree for Majok. They strung lights, and hung ornaments. There had been the funeral dirge but now everyone sang out with brightly lit faces. Majok got his final wish. And in places around Cleveland, Ohio people were learning a little bit about their neighbors.

999

Since 1992, UNICEF has reunited nearly 1,200 boys and girls with their families. Approximately 17,000 remain in camps.

What is Going on Now in Sudan?

"South Sudan is going through one of the most difficult times since the signing in January 2005 of the Comprehensive Peace Agreement (CPA) between the Sudan People's Liberation Movement (SPLM) and the Government of Sudan…"

so begins an article from October 12, 2009 at the site **http://www.gurtong.net** --a very good place to find out all you can.

In the article the United Nations estimates that the conflict in southern Sudan has taken over 2, 000 lives.

It says 250,000 people have been forced away from their homes *since January this year.*

"The fatality tally according to the report outnumbers that in the war- ravaged Darfur…"

Sources

**Especially the personal accounts of Cleveland
Sudanese Lost Boys Akol Ayii Madut, Dominic Deng
Mel & Aleu Akot Athuai**

Encyclopedia of Cleveland History http://ech.cwru.edu

"NBA Star Now Refugee": http://www.focusdep.com

http://www.allianceforthelostboys.com

http://www.ethiopianreview.com

http://en.wikipedia.org/wiki/Lost_Boys_of_Sudan

http://southsudanfriends.org

http://www.cleveland.com/brett/blog/index.ssf/lost_boys
_of_sudan/

http://www.unicef.org

Some Notable Sudanese

Francis Bok   author and abolitionist

Manute Bol   former NBA player/activist

Luol Deng   NBA basketball player

Valentino Achak Deng   subject of David Eggers'
fictionalized biography *What is the What*

Deng Gai   former NBA player

Emmanuel Jal   hip hop artist and memoirist

Mijok Lang aka Hot Dogg   rapper

Taban lo Liyong   poet

Alek wek   supermodel

To Read and To Watch

The Lost Boy: The true story of a young boy's flight from Sudan to South Africa by Aher Arop Bol 2009

The Lost Boys of Sudan by Mark Bixler 2005

God Grew Tired of Us: A Memoir by John Bul Dau and Michael Sweeney 2007

They Poured Fire On Us From The Sky by Alephonsion Deng, Benson Deng, and Benjamin Ajak (Edited by Judy A. Bernstein) 2005

What is the What The Autobiography of Valentino Achak Deng by David Eggers 2006

The Journey of the Lost Boys by Joan Hecht 2005

Lost Boy No More by DiAnn Mills and Abraham Nhial 2004

Lost Boys of Sudan an Emmy nominated film aired on the PBS series P.O.V. by Megan Mylan and Jon Shenk 2003

God Grew Tired of Us (a documentary film preceding Dau's memoirs) by Christopher Dillon Quinn 2006